This Little Tiger book belongs to:

_____

_____

_____

To my friend, Nick

LITTLE TIGER PRESS LTD,
an imprint of the Little Tiger Group
1 The Coda Centre, 189 Munster Road, London SW6 6AW
www.littletiger.co.uk

First published in Great Britain 2005
This edition published 2016

Text and illustrations copyright © Ruth Galloway 2005
Ruth Galloway has asserted her right to be identified as the author and illustrator
of this work under the Copyright, Designs and Patents Act, 1988
A CIP catalogue record for this book is available from the British Library

All rights reserved • ISBN 978-1-84869-501-6

Printed in China • LTP/1400/1892/0417

2 4 6 8 10 9 7 5 3 1

Clumsy Crab

Ruth Galloway

LiTTLE TiGER

LONDON

Nipper the crab hated his huge
clumsy claws. However hard he tried
they always got in the way.

None of his friends had
clumsy claws. He wished he had tickly
tentacles like Octopus and Jellyfish, or
flippety fins like Turtle and the fish.

One day Nipper was playing
catch the bubble with his friends.

POP!

His clumsy claws
pricked the bubble
and it burst.

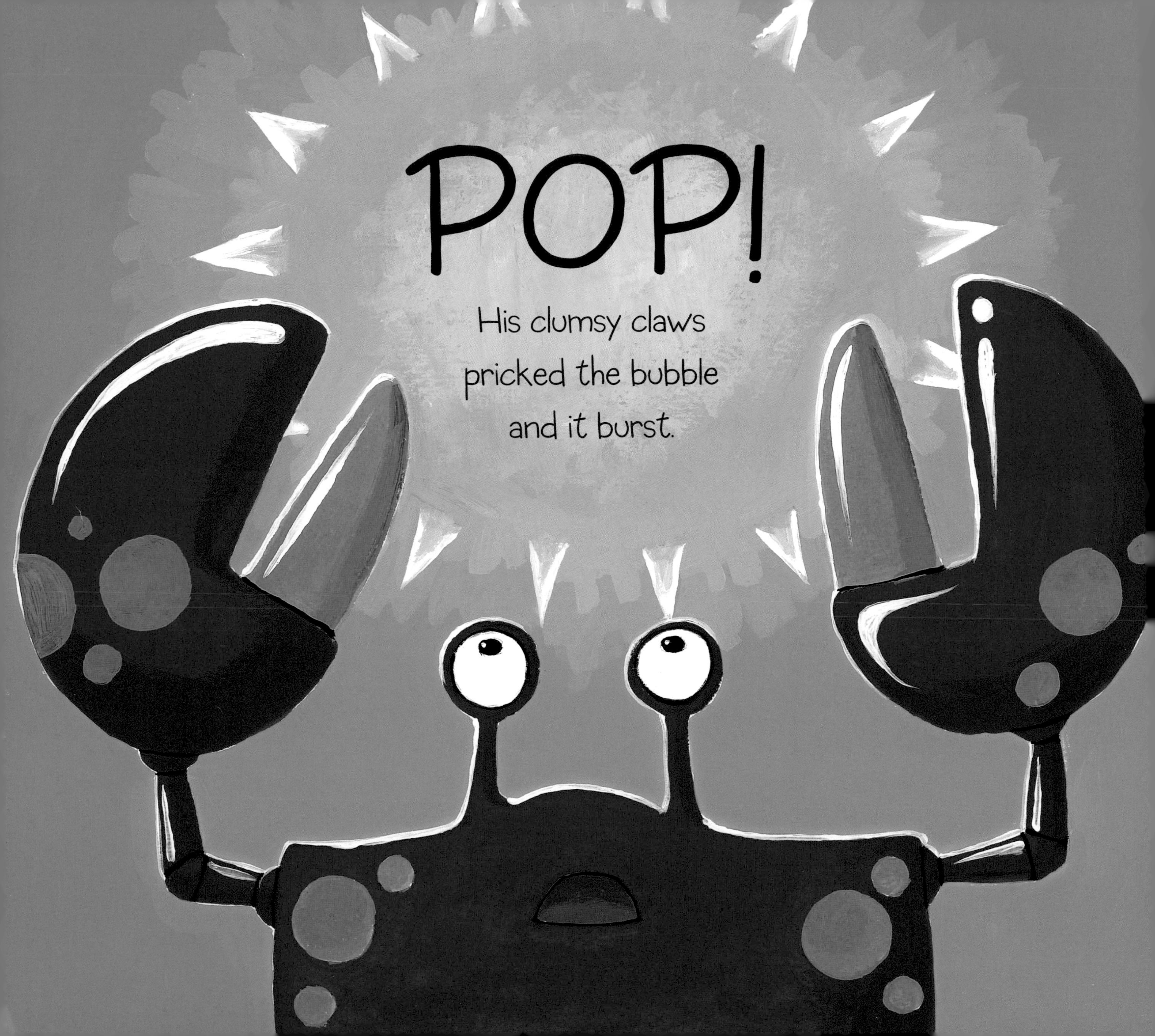

They couldn't play
that game any more. They
played chase instead.

Nipper scuttled off sideways,
but one of his clumsy claws got in the way.

He slipped and stumbled,
tripped and tumbled until . . .

. . . he was buried up to his eyes
in sand. Turtle had to dig him out.

They all decided to play hide and seek. Crab climbed into a big clam shell and pulled it shut.

It was the
PERFECT
hiding place. Until . . .

CRACK!

. . . Nipper's clumsy claws shattered
the shell into hundreds of tiny pieces.
"Ouch!" he cried.

Nipper sighed. "If only I didn't have
these claws I'd be good at hide and seek."
"Don't worry, Nipper," said Jellyfish, picking up the
pieces of shell. "We'll hide, and you can find us."

Nipper counted to ten
then set off to find his
friends. He searched in the
sand . . . and found Turtle.

He searched
under the shells . . .
and found Jellyfish.

He searched up and down and in and out of rocks . . .

but he couldn't find
Octopus anywhere.

Then they heard a cry.
Octopus was tightly tangled
in some seaweed.

Help!

Octopus squirmed and squiggled
and wriggled and jiggled. Turtle and
Jellyfish tried to help, but the knots just
got tighter and tighter.

Nipper had an idea.

He gently snipped at the seaweed with his claws and small pieces floated away. Faster and faster Nipper danced around the clump of seaweed.

His claws moved quickly, slashing and slicing, shredding and dicing, until the sea was filled with pieces of seaweed swirling all around.

Octopus was finally free!
"Thank you, you clever crab!" he cheered.
Nipper waved his claws happily. At last
he knew how useful they could be.

More fabulous books from Little Tiger Press!

Fidgety Fish
Ruth Galloway

Gillian Lobel
Little Honey Bear and the Smiley Moon
Tim Warnes

STEVE SMALLMAN
THE LAMB WHO CAME FOR DINNER

Click Clack Crocodile's Back
Kathryn White   Joëlle Dreidemy

Puppy's First Christmas

The Very Busy Day
Diana Hendry   Jane Chapman

For information regarding any of the above titles
or for our catalogue, please contact us:
Little Tiger Press, 1 The Coda Centre,
189 Munster Road, London SW6 6AW
Tel: 020 7385 6333
E-mail: contact@littletiger.co.uk
www.littletiger.co.uk